MAGIC and Illusion

My sincere thanks to the following people for their time, information, images and enthusiasm for this book:

Lee Cohen, Melbourne, Australia

Tim Mason and his family, Melbourne, Australia

Simon Coronel, Melbourne, Australia

Tim Ellis, Melbourne, Australia

ABC 3 production crew, Melbourne, Australia.

Dear Reader

The skill and artistry of magicians and illusionists can suspend our sense of reality, if only for a moment in time. They invite us on a journey of magical wonder and entertainment and, while working on this book, that's exactly what I experienced!

I had the privilege of meeting three of the industry's most talented magicians and illusionists – Lee Cohen, Tim Mason and Simon Coronel. At the time, they were juggling busy performance schedules for Australian and international audiences, yet they graciously carved out time to help me with this book.

AT FIRST, I HAD THE WORST STAGE FRIGHT IN THE WORLD!

LEE COHEN

I hope you enjoy finding out about some of the fastidious planning and rehearsals involved, as the magicians prepare seamless and fascinating performances that thrill and entertain audiences.

Sharon Parsons

NELSON
CENGAGE Learning™
For learning solutions, visit cengage.com.au

Contents

Magic and Illusion

1 Magician, Lee Cohen

Historically, in the world of magic, men have usually been the magicians and women have been their assistants. Today, the stage lights beam down on a growing number of female magicians.

One of them is Lee Cohen, who performs her magic in Melbourne, Australia, and around the world. If you're lucky enough to see Lee perform on the stage, you'll understand why audiences love her special style of magic.

Lee Cohen holds her rabbit, Muffin. Lee is the current president of the Australian Institute of Magic.

Lee Assisted her Dad

As a young girl of eight, Lee became fascinated with magic when she was an assistant for her magician father. She especially enjoyed watching her father produce a rabbit from inside something, like a cake tin. Lee loved the art of magic so much that she decided to work as a magician from the age of 16.

Lee Explains Magic Terms

Magic or Illusion?

Q: Some people call themselves "magicians" and others prefer the term "illusionists". What is the difference between magic and illusion?

A: Magic is the overall performance art form and illusion is a genre of magic.

Tricks or Effects?

Q: Do you use the term "magic tricks"?

A: Yes, "magic tricks" is acceptable but we prefer to use the term "magic effects", because we're not trying to trick people but entertain them with magical experiences.

Big-Stage or Close-Up?

Q: What are the main kinds of magic performance?

A: There are many forms of magic performance, but most magicians specialise in either big-stage or close-up magic.

> "MAGIC IS NOT CREEPY, IT'S A CRAFT LIKE ANY OTHER ART FORM."
>
> LEE COHEN

2 Success in Magic

Purple Is Lee's Signature Colour!

Lee Cohen is a successful magician, but it has taken her many years of learning to perfect the craft of magic.

A big part of performing magic is working out how best to present the effects so that they entertain and intrigue the audience. Lee has achieved that goal with style, perfect timing and an engaging personality.

Anxious at First

When Lee recalls her first public performance, she says, "I felt anxious and I thought I'd never get through it. So I quickly reminded myself that I had practised my performance until it was perfect at home, and I was fine. That experience was so good for my confidence. I had more fun at my next magic show and now I'm addicted to performing magic to anyone at any time and … anywhere!"

> "IT IS A PRIVILEGE TO PERFORM MY MAGIC AND TAKE PEOPLE TO A PLACE WHERE THEY CAN STILL BELIEVE IN THE POWER OF MAGIC."
>
> LEE COHEN

Lee's Tips for Beginners

Observe the Experts

Magicians are always learning and perfecting their craft, and they are keen observers of great illusions and effects performed by other magicians. Anyone interested in becoming a magician should spend a lot of time observing skilled magicians and illusionists.

Practise to Perfect

Once a magician has learned a new magic effect, it has to be practised over and over again until it's a perfectly polished performance.

Adaptable in Magic

Magicians must be adaptable because they have to work in different venues and at special occasions, and perform for diverse audiences.

Unique Magic

It is the aim of every magician to captivate an audience with unique and creative magic effects that leave them wondering, "How did she do that magic trick?"

Creating Magic Effects

Creative works that can be used to make a profit are known as intellectual property. Magicians who create a new effect can legally patent it, or protect it. This means that other magicians must pay a performance fee to the creator of the magic effect. A magician must buy the rights from the creator of a magic effect before they can publically perform it. This allows the person who created the intellectual property to share in the profits made by another person who performs that magic effect.

"FOR THE AUDIENCE, IT'S MORE ENTERTAINING WHEN THEY DON'T KNOW HOW THE MAGIC EFFECTS WERE DONE.

LEE COHEN"

3 Lee's "Magic" Pets

Lee loves animals and involves some of her pets in her magic performances. However, she says that they are her pets first and performers second. Lee has a good understanding of her pets' personalities and talents, so she decides which animal will work best in each kind of performance.

Star Rabbits

Hunny Bunny is a six-month-old Holland lop rabbit and he is very shy, so Lee does not allow children to handle him at a performance. Instead, Lee holds him in the comfort and security of a deep, soft felt hat.

On the other hand, Muffin, her eight-year-old French lop rabbit, is the star attraction at most of Lee's shows for children. After a show, Muffin is used to being patted by audience members.

Norman E Normous is a New Zealand white rabbit, who will soon make appearances in Lee's magic shows to give Muffin a holiday from time to time.

Hunny Bunny snuggles into Lee's magic hat.

Lee gets the full attention of Muffin before going on stage.

Magician's Doves

Lee has eight white doves that feature in her magic shows. The doves that magicians use are often known as ringneck doves, ringdoves or Barbary doves.

Lee with Boomer

Lee's Magic Performance Tips

During each performance, Lee suggests that a magician should:

1. talk enthusiastically to the audience to help make them feel relaxed and engaged
2. present magic effects with perfect timing and style to hold the audience's attention
3. tell a story to support the magic effect and to keep the audience engaged. A story Lee tells is: "Boomer, my dove, is missing and I've been looking everywhere for him." *(Lee lifts several boxes to show the audience that he is not under any of them.)* "Oh dear, I wonder where Boomer is?" *(Boomer magically appears under one of the empty boxes.)* "Boomer, how did you get in there?" exclaims Lee.

4 A Clown's Magic Show

One of Lee Cohen's many magical characters is Kobi the Clown. Lee's assistants are her pet rabbits and doves, which magically appear throughout the show.

Arts

Make-Up, Costume Design and Acting

Lee has created many characters, who enable her to perform for different audiences. Lee's background in make-up artistry and costume design provides her with the skills to create colourful characters. Her acting experience helps her to perform in public with clarity, confidence and humour.

Lee makes balloon animals to help young children feel comfortable with her character.

Kobi the Clown in....

Kobi's Magical Menagerie!

Plan and Prepare

Before every magic show, Lee spends a lot of time planning and preparing so she can present a professional performance.

Pre-Performance

The children in an audience can range from preschoolers to teenagers. When Lee is performing to very young children, she begins the show with a warm-up activity to help them feel comfortable and trust her as a performer.

Performance Personality

Once the audience is settled, Lee's naturally warm personality puts the children at ease as she involves them in her show by asking questions and inviting them to join her on stage.

Pretend and Prove

Lee's clown character cleverly builds intrigue by pretending to get certain magic effects wrong. Sometimes Lee performs a magic effect in such a way that the children think they know how she has done it. Lee will say, "You know how I did the trick?" The kids will call out "Yes!" to which Lee will reply, "Do you *really* know how I did the trick?" Again the kids will call out "Yes!" Then one child explains how Lee did the trick. So Lee repeats the magic effect and proves that they were wrong. The audience erupts into applause.

Lee gives an animated performance.

"I'm so sad that the show is over!"

> ON BUSY DAYS I ASK MYSELF, 'WHO AM I TODAY?'
>
> LEE COHEN

Pack Up

When the audience has left and the stage is quiet, Lee packs up everything so she can drive to her next performance. But which character will she be … a clown, a pirate, a fairy or a storybook character?

"In you go, Norman. It's only a short ride to the next show."

"All packed up and ready for the next show."

Post-Performance

At the end of each performance, Lee invites the children and their parents to join her on stage to ask questions and pat her pets.

HISTORY FEATURE

A Hero for Many Magicians

Robert-Houdin

Many magicians and illusionists around the world recognise Jean Eugène Robert-Houdin as the "father of modern magic". More about this talented magician is revealed in Chapter 12.

The House of Magic

Go to the House of Magic (*La Maison de la Magie*) in Blois, France, and you will enter a world of illusions. Visitors learn about the life and work of Jean Eugène Robert-Houdin, experience an interactive area of magic arts, robots and optical games, and meet entertaining magicians.

Lee stands next to a statue of Robert-Houdin at La Maison de la Magie.

Lee at Robert-Houdin's Home

Lee is honoured to visit this private property, which was once home to Robert-Houdin.

Lee visits the museum at the House of Magic.

Lee reads the historic plaque about Robert-Houdin.

5 Lee Takes her Magic to South Africa

Lee urges fellow magician Simon Coronel to volunteer to get inside the box but he isn't sure he wants to be sliced into thirds!

A Fundraising Magic Show

In 2012, Lee attended the College of Magic in Cape Town, South Africa, where she worked as a volunteer with students for two months.

Before Lee could go to South Africa, she had to raise some extra money, so her fellow magicians and illusionists volunteered their time to put on an amazing magic show for families and friends. One of the illusions in the show featured Lee and her illusionist friend, Simon Coronel. (Simon "reappears" in Chapter 11.)

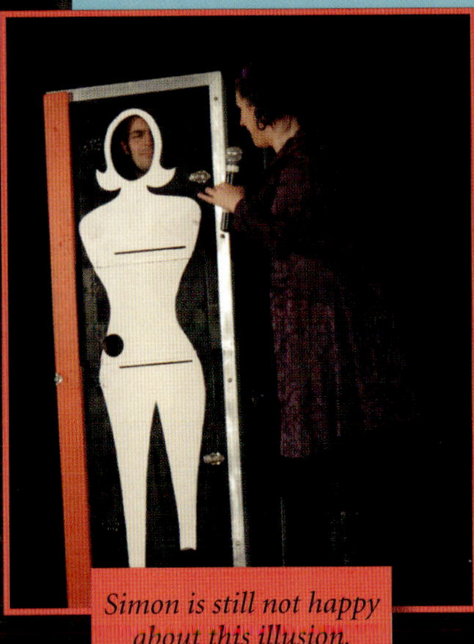

Simon is still not happy about this illusion.

Simon can't believe that his midsection has disappeared!

Simon's body is whole again but he's still a bit "sore"!

Lee at the College of Magic in South Africa

Lee and the students after a face art lesson

Lee assists students as they learn to make balloon animals.

6 Inside Tim's Magic Room

The magic room of 12-year-old magician Tim Mason is a treasure trove filled with props and equipment that help him to create wondrous magic effects.

Tim is an extraordinary magician with a natural ability to perform magical illusions. He prefers to call them illusions or magic effects – not magic tricks – because his art form involves a skilled and swift sleight of hand to create an optical illusion for an audience.

Tim has a sharp eye for working out the sleight-of-hand movements required to perform various illusions, but this still involves hours of practice.

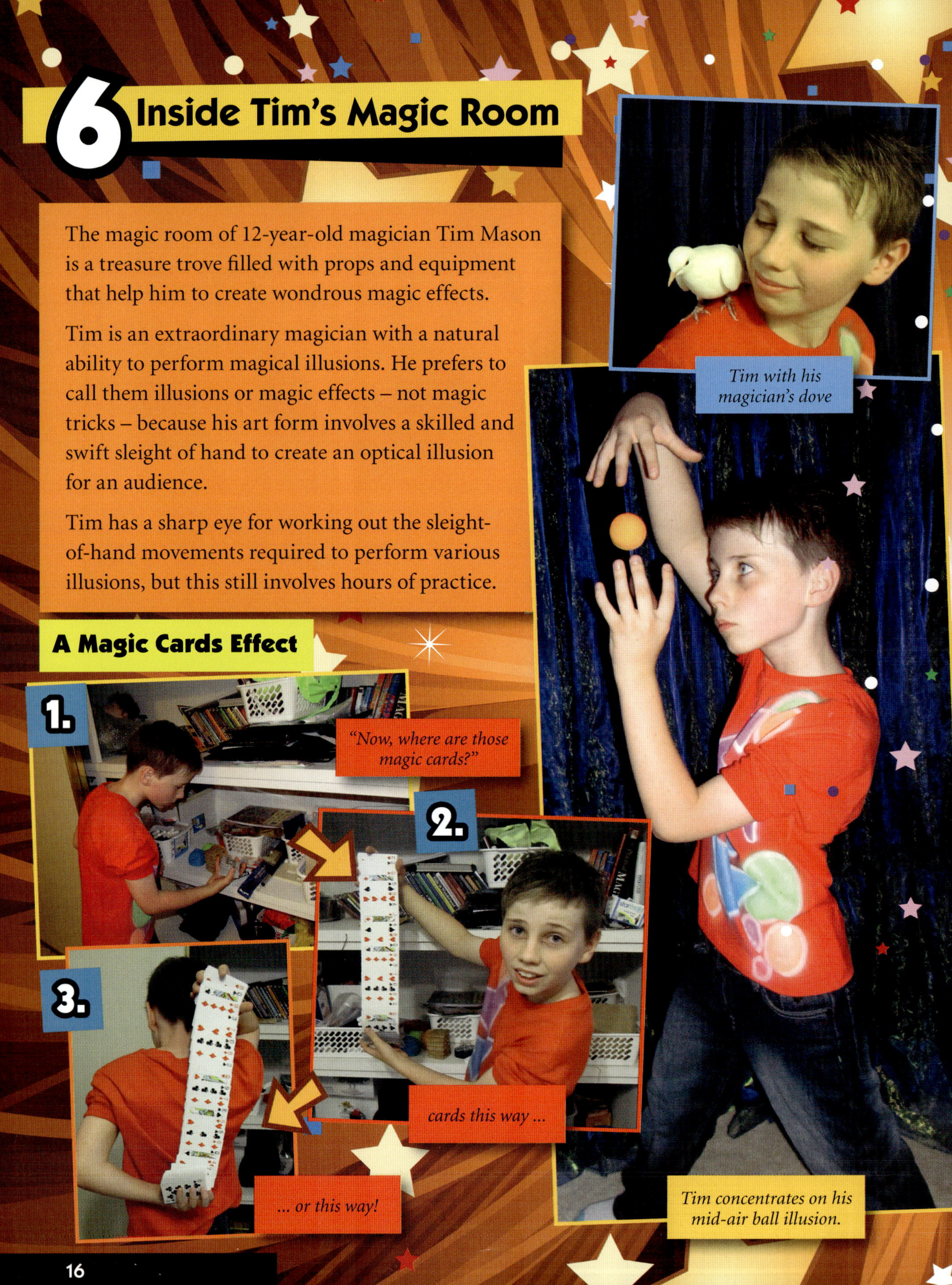

Tim with his magician's dove

A Magic Cards Effect

1. "Now, where are those magic cards?"

2. cards this way ...

3. ... or this way!

Tim concentrates on his mid-air ball illusion.

A Magic Box Effect

1. "Found the magic box!"

2. "I open one panel before putting in my hand to show that nothing is inside."

3. "See, nothing is inside."

4. "After I blow on the box, a red ball magically appears."

5. "Then I focus on the red ball before blowing on it again."

6. "After I blow on the box, the red ball magically disappears."

7. "I am happy when my magic effect is successful."

7 Tim's Magical Journey

Magic from Five

Tim Mason began his magic journey at preschool and since that time he has practised diligently in preparation for every performance. Tim takes great pride in performing professionally for family and friends, for public audiences, and for teachers and students at school. He says, "I have been lucky that my school supported my love of magic and illusions."

Tim introduces his magic effect at preschool.

magic at preschool

a magic effect for the school principal

> "IT'S HILARIOUS WHEN ADULTS SAY, 'WHOA, HOW DID HE DO THAT?'"
> TIM MASON

Tim at an outdoor magic performance

Tim's magic awards

Lee Cohen congratulates Tim on winning his magic awards.

Magical Choreography

Tim often performs his magic to music, but he needs to ensure that every one of his movements matches the music. The entire performance has to be choreographed so that the audience views a seamless performance of magical illusion and music. An important part of a perfectly choreographed performance is allowing time for the audience to participate or respond. A laugh, a gasp and applause are music to the ears of a magician!

1. *"My magic rings effect starts with two rings. I can join the two rings and then slide them apart."*

2. *"Then I put a third magic ring on my shoulder, ready for my three-ring effect."*

A Magic Rings Effect

3. *"In a split second, the three rings become three joined rings."*

4. *"And then the effect finishes with four rings joined around my body."*

8 Magic Builds Tim's Confidence

Tim says, "When I'm on stage it feels nerve-racking for the first 20 seconds, but as soon as I hear an appreciative audience clapping, I feel great! There are many skills that I have been taught by my magic teachers, which have helped to build my confidence. Here are some of them."

1. Practise, Practise, Practise!

Tim works with a magic teacher every week and then spends hours practising at home.

2. Audience Participation

A great way to maintain the audience's attention is to invite someone to become involved in a magic effect.

3. Engage the Audience

Think about a captivating story to narrate throughout the performance that will capture and hold the audience's attention.

4. If Something Goes Wrong

Keep your cool and continue with the performance.

5. A Hazard-Free Environment

Only perform in a carefully arranged environment to minimise any chance of mistakes during the magic performance.

6. Humour

Build humour into the performance – the patter, the magic effect and body language.

Lee Cohen often teaches Tim and in this magic illusion, she is teaching him about levitation.

Something Went Wrong

During Tim's "Hippity Hoppity Rabbits" magic effect, some of the props fell apart, but he proceeded in a professional manner. At the end, the audience still clapped and that boosted Tim's confidence even though he was disappointed that the effect didn't work.

Smiles for Tim

"The smiles on kids' faces really spur me on to do my best magic!" says Tim.

Magical Benefits

From a young age, Tim has performed his illusions to a wide variety of audiences at celebratory occasions, on television, and at indoor and outdoor stage settings. Some of the benefits that he has gained are described below.

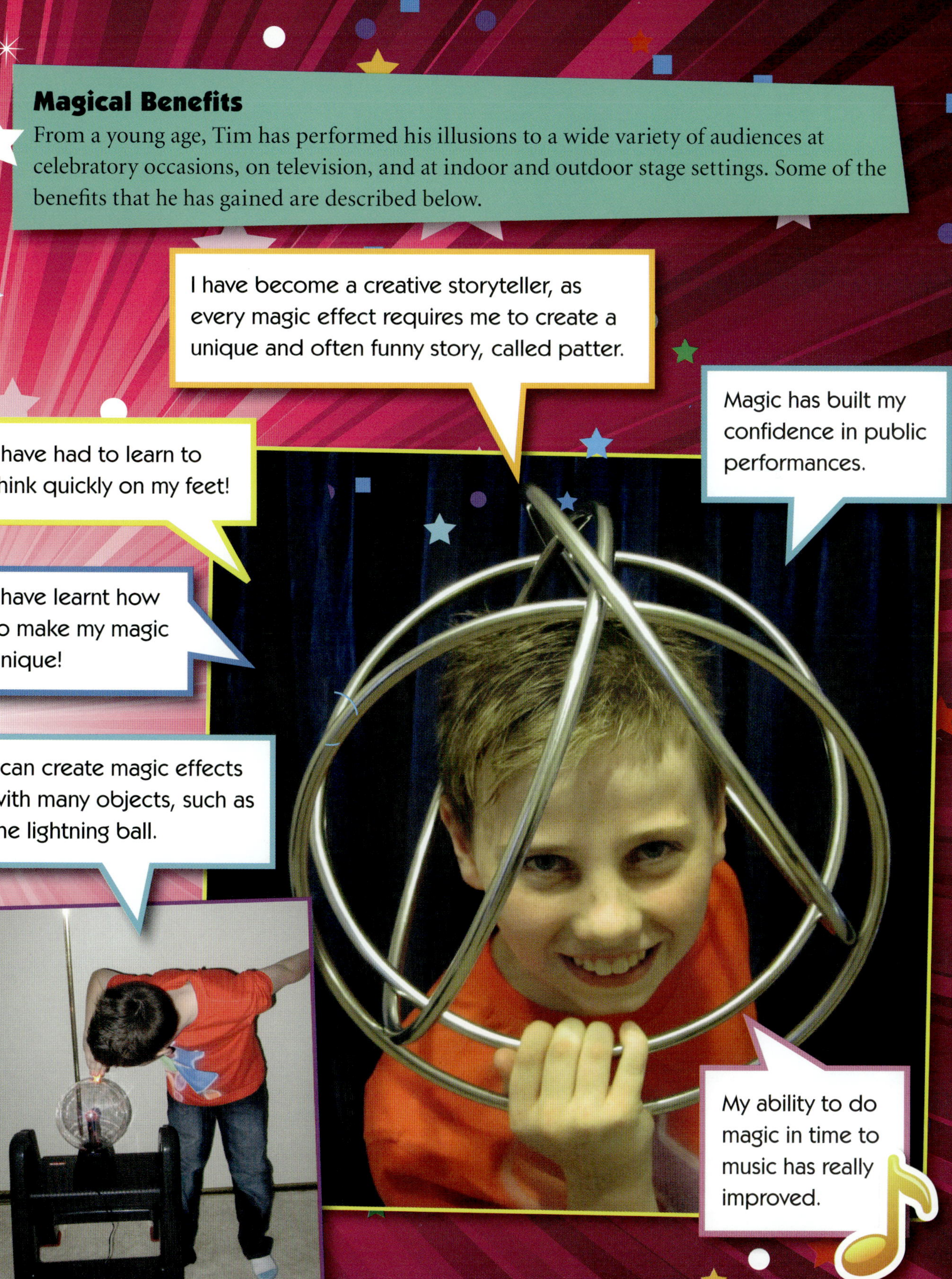

9 Tim on TV

At the age of 12, Tim Mason was invited to appear on television programs, such as *Young Talent Time,* and the television channel, ABC 3. After more than six years in the business of magic, these invitations honour and reward the high level of performance that Tim has achieved.

On-Set Support

Tim with his family and Lee Cohen

Organise Props

Tim gets props ready for filming.

Rehearsals

Tim gets directions from the ABC 3 television producer.

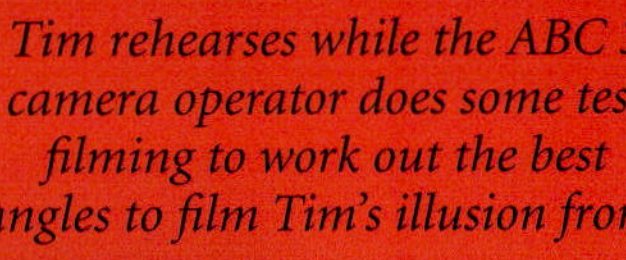

Tim rehearses while the ABC 3 camera operator does some test filming to work out the best angles to film Tim's illusion from

Tim gets instructions from one of his teachers, Tim Ellis, before the camera rolls.

Ready, Action, Magic

The illusion begins with Tim explaining that there is nothing inside Robal; he then lifts the back flap to prove that there is nothing inside the little truck.

After Tim has twirled Robal around in front of the cameras, he lifts the lid to magically reveal his brother, Blair.

Pack Up

Tim's Family Meets David Copperfield

After Tim won the 2009 Australian Junior Magic Championships for the categories of "Close-up" and "Big-stage", Tim's aunt emailed David Copperfield about his success. To Tim's surprise, David Copperfield arranged second-row seats and backstage passes at his Australian show. Tim says, "I was awestruck!"

David Copperfield (centre) with Tim's mother and Tim (left), and Tim's brother and father (right).

For more information on David Copperfield, see pages 24–25.

10 A Famous Big-Stage Illusionist

Most illusions are performed on a big stage and one of the most famous big-stage illusionists is David Copperfield (1956–). David began performing magic when he was only 12 years old, and is now one of the highest-paid entertainers in the world.

Magic Milestones

David Copperfield has enjoyed many career milestones. At the age of 22, he had a television show called *The Magic of David Copperfield*. When David was 27 years old, he made New York City's famous Statue of Liberty "disappear" for a matter of seconds.

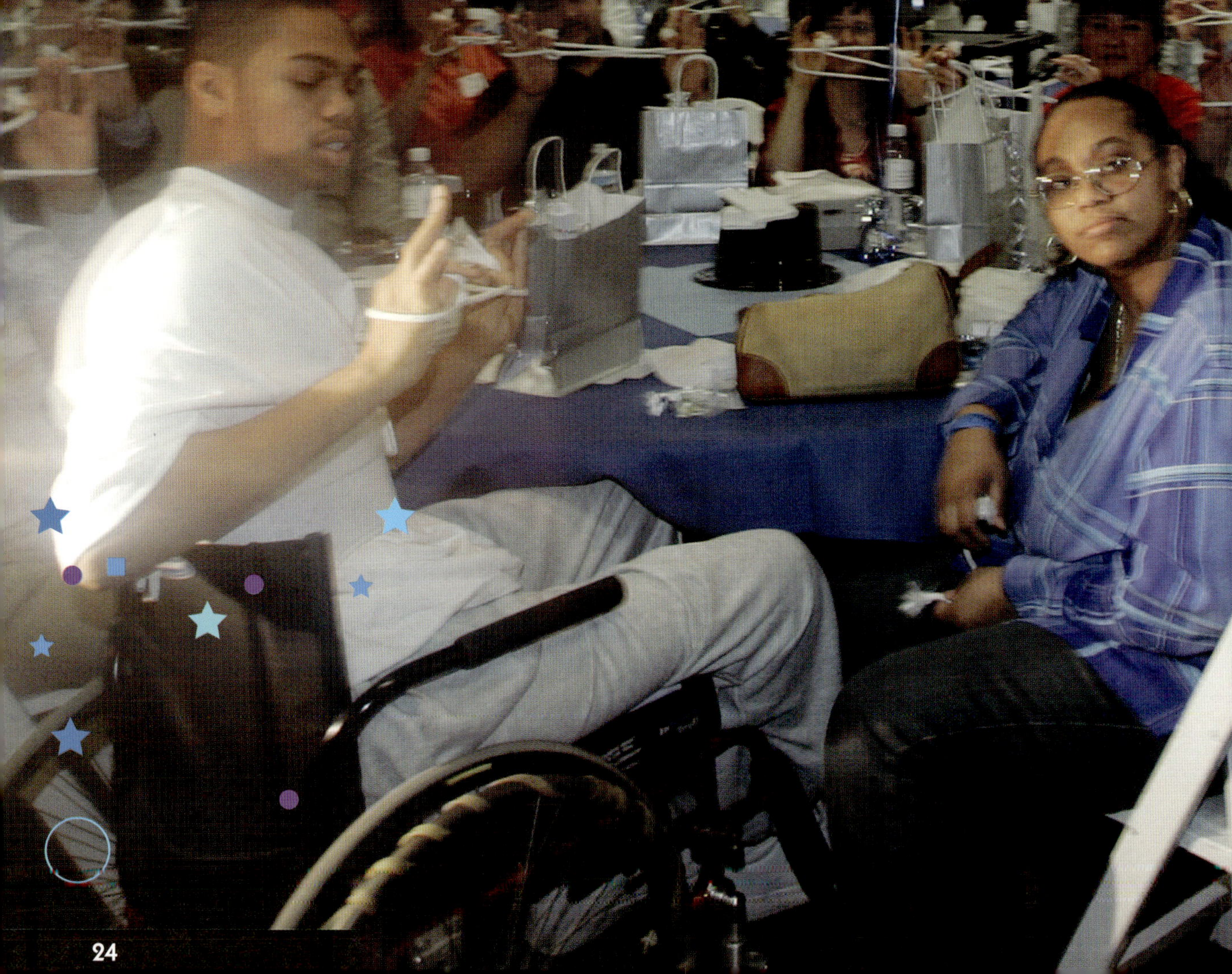

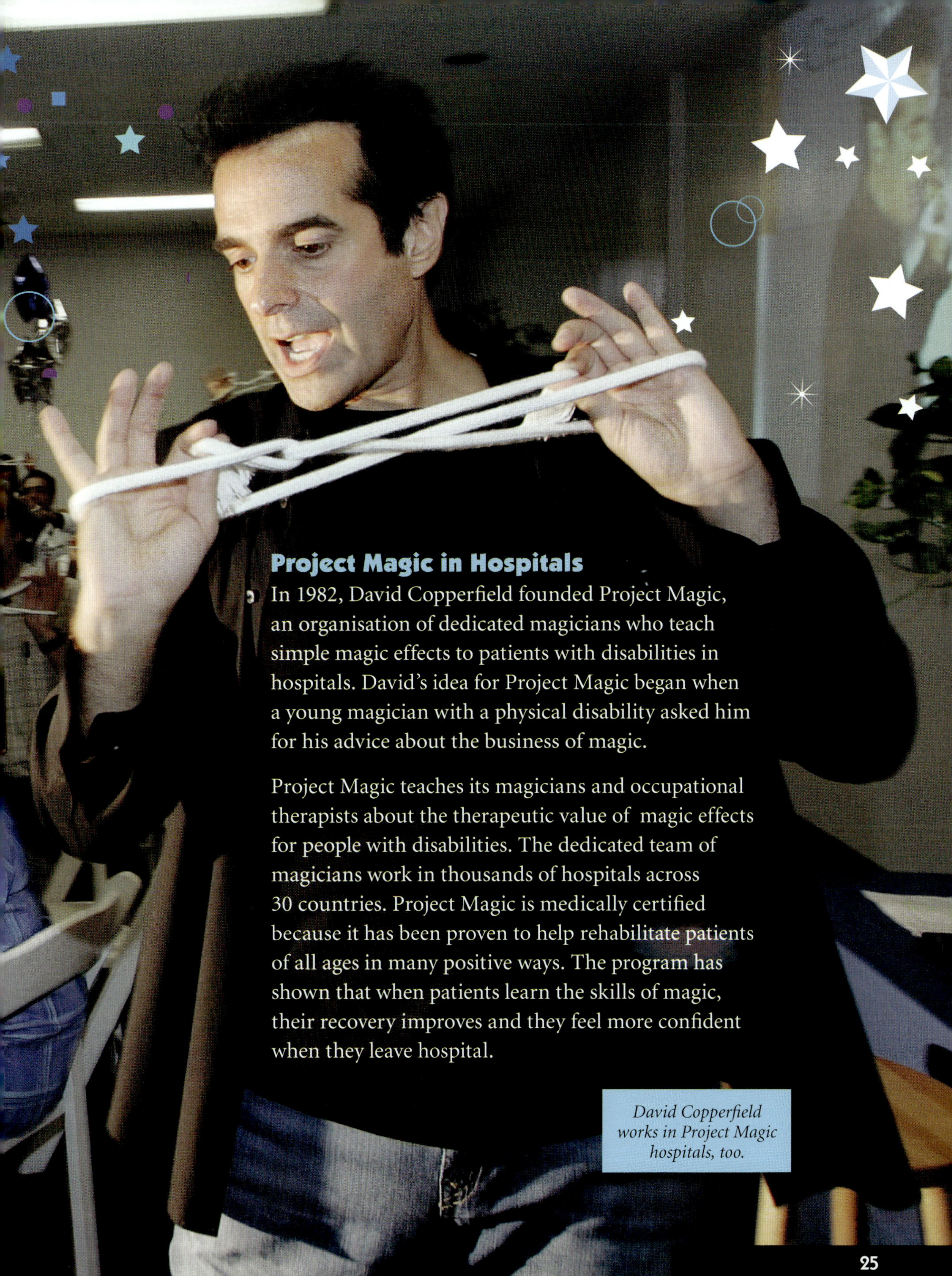

Project Magic in Hospitals

In 1982, David Copperfield founded Project Magic, an organisation of dedicated magicians who teach simple magic effects to patients with disabilities in hospitals. David's idea for Project Magic began when a young magician with a physical disability asked him for his advice about the business of magic.

Project Magic teaches its magicians and occupational therapists about the therapeutic value of magic effects for people with disabilities. The dedicated team of magicians work in thousands of hospitals across 30 countries. Project Magic is medically certified because it has been proven to help rehabilitate patients of all ages in many positive ways. The program has shown that when patients learn the skills of magic, their recovery improves and they feel more confident when they leave hospital.

David Copperfield works in Project Magic hospitals, too.

11 A World-Championship Illusionist

Simon Coronel is a close-up illusionist who lives in Melbourne, Australia. While Simon was a first-year university student, he experienced his first magic effect. He says, "I was so fascinated by magical illusions, I felt compelled to try and understand how they worked."

Simon says, "Close-up illusion is when a performer makes seemingly impossible things happen up close by using their sleight-of-hand skills."

Simon is the only Australian in over a decade (and the fourth Australian ever) to win a prize at the International Federation of Magic Societies World Championships of Magic.

Simon Coronel begins his amazing sleight-of-hand illusion with a card.

Simon integrates his illusions into a motivational talk for university students.

Arts

International Magic Organisation

The International Federation of Magic Societies (FISM) is an organisation that runs the biggest magic competition in the world. Every three years (since 1952), FISM has presented the World Championships of Magic. It is a prestigious event that many magicians aspire to attend in order to present their special style of magic or illusion.

Many of Simon's illusions use playing cards.

Convincing Illusions

To create a convincing illusion, Simon must invest several months into practising and perfecting his series of sleight-of-hand movements, with cards, coins and notes. While performing his illusions, Simon also creates patter that captures and holds the interest of an audience by cleverly weaving in humour and fun.

Simon especially enjoys teaching people how to present their illusions in a confident and convincing style, too.

Simon presents his illusions at a business conference.

Simon involves attendees in his illusions at the business conference.

> "IT'S WONDERFUL TO DO SOMETHING THAT LOOKS IMPOSSIBLE BUT ISN'T."
>
> SIMON CORONEL

ILLUSION EFFECTS

When Simon uses a coin, he can perform all kinds of illusion effects with his skilful sleight-of-hand movements.

Production

MAKE A COIN SUDDENLY APPEAR in the fingers or hand.

Vanish

MAKE A COIN SUDDENLY DISAPPEAR in the fingers or hand.

Reproduction

MAKE A COIN SUDDENLY REAPPEAR in the fingers or hand.

Transposition

MAKE A COIN GO FROM ONE LOCATION TO ANOTHER, e.g. appear in one hand and then reappear in the other hand.

Penetration

MAKE A COIN GO THROUGH THE CLOTH OF A JACKET AND REAPPEAR in another part of the jacket.

Transformation

MAKE A COIN SUDDENLY CHANGE INTO SOMETHING ELSE, e.g. a five-dollar note, or change its shape or size.

12 World's Most Influential Illusionist – Robert-Houdin or Houdini?

Robert-Houdin

Jean Eugène Robert-Houdin was a French clockmaker. One day, a book on magic was delivered to him instead of a book on clockmaking, and that changed his life. From that moment, he avidly read books about science, and the concepts he learnt about helped him to perform amazing magic shows.

Robert-Houdin performs a "disappearing woman" effect.

Science

Secret to the Adapted "Light and Heavy Chest" Effect

Robert-Houdin invited three members of the audience to lift the small wooden box, using a pulley system, and to keep hold of the rope. When the assistant turned on the magnet, the electromagnetic force caused the box to drop to the floor and the three men to be miraculously lifted up.

Secret to the First "Light and Heavy Chest" Effect

For the "Light and Heavy Chest" effect, Robert-Houdin invited a member of the audience to lift a small wooden box (that contained his money) and then put it back down on the stage floor. Then he instructed the box to stay on the stage so that no one could steal his money. When Robert-Houdin asked the same person to lift the box again, it was "too heavy" to lift. The secret? Inside the box was a metal plate and an electromagnet was hidden under the floor directly beneath the box. Therefore, when Robert-Houdin's assistant turned on the magnet, the strong force made it impossible to lift.

Houdini Influenced by Robert-Houdin

Three years after Robert-Houdin died, Harry Houdini was born in Hungary – his family later moved to the USA. When Houdini was a teenager, he was so inspired by Robert-Houdin's autobiography that he began a magic career at 17 years of age. Houdini's birth name was Erik Weisz, but he changed his name to Harry Houdini after he read Robert-Houdin's autobiography.

Houdini's Famous Acts

As Houdini's fame grew, so did the complexity of his acts. Houdini's famous escapology acts involved him freeing himself from locked handcuffs, chains and locks, often while underwater or inside crates.

History

Houdini First to Fly a Plane in Australia

Houdini was the first person to fly a plane in Australia. In 1910, he flew for some minutes in Diggers Rest near Melbourne. Although his performances were in Melbourne, it is said that he slept under the plane, hoping for better flying weather.

DISCUSSION FEATURE

Who Was the World's Most Influential Illusionist – Robert-Houdin or Houdini?

Jean Eugène Robert-Houdin (1805–1871) and Harry Houdini (1874–1926) are regarded as two of the most famous experts in magic and illusion. Both were inspired to become magicians through their reading. Although their acts were significantly different, each magician developed new approaches to the performance of magical illusions, and consequently had a major influence on how magic has since been performed. But which magician was the more influential illusionist?

Jean Eugène Robert-Houdin

Jean Eugène Robert-Houdin's performances of magic changed the way that magic is performed today. He took magic performances from the street to the stage. He also started the trend of dressing in a suit to look more professional. As a result of his innovations, the public began viewing the art of magic as a credible profession.

Robert-Houdin also added significantly to the abilities of magicians by developing new acts, which others later learnt and adapted. He used his mechanical experience as a clockmaker and his knowledge of scientific concepts to create never-before-seen illusions on stage. At the time, his audiences were amazed at the spectacular and seemingly inexplicable performances. One of his most famous illusions, called the "Light and Heavy Chest", was based on electromagnetism, which had only recently been discovered and was largely unknown to the general public.

Robert-Houdin's understanding of mechanics also enabled him to build lifelike mechanical figures, known as automatons. These included figures that wrote and drew, played instruments or danced on a tightrope. In a time when all-metal machines were relatively new, his inventions astounded many people.

Perhaps Robert-Houdin's biggest achievement resulted from a request by the French government, who wanted him to use his skills in French-occupied Algeria to help quell the unrest there. He used his magical illusions to convince the Algerians that the French had greater powers than those of the local leaders.

Although his career as a magician spanned only 11 years, Robert-Houdin's scientifically based magic enthralled audiences of all classes and ages. His acts have had an undeniable influence on his successors, transforming how magical illusion has been performed ever since.

Harry Houdini

Harry Houdini is another world-renowned magician who created his own style of magic and had enormous influence on how illusions were later performed. Like Robert-Houdin, Houdini used his early skills to enhance his performances. As a youth, he was a champion athlete and practised acrobatics. He used his fitness to undertake amazing physical feats of endurance, such as staying underwater for lengthy periods or dangling from a rope off a building the . As a young man, he worked as a locksmith's apprentice, and developed an understanding of locking mechanisms, which was invaluable for picking locks.

Houdini started his performance career doing magic card tricks, but he wasn't successful. So he became an illusionist and took his performance off the stage to some of the most dangerous and unbelievable places around the world.

Houdini was the first person in history to popularise the art of escapology and is arguably the greatest escapologist of all time. Houdini's skills were such that by the early 1900s, he had become one of the highest paid entertainers in Europe, earning about US$2000 per week. Many of Houdini's acts of escapology involved escaping from chains, handcuffs or a tight straitjacket, often while hanging from a rope. At other times he performed in extremely dangerous situations, such as while inside a water-filled container, which added the thrill of suspense and built his reputation for death-defying acts.

Through his work with the Society of American Magicians, Houdini helped to improve the public perception of magicians as professional performers. His escapes were legendary and his influence on the art of illusion was substantial.

The Walrus Decides

Both Jean Eugène Robert-Houdin and Harry Houdini thrilled audiences with their ability to seemingly achieve the impossible. Robert-Houdin's use of science enabled him to perform acts that appeared inexplicable, whereas Houdini's daring-do and powers of physical endurance gave the impression of superhuman powers. By applying their consummate skills in performance, they not only built on earlier acts but substantially advanced the profession of magicians. Houdini had a long career in Europe and the USA, which has perhaps made him more memorable among the public. However, Robert-Houdin, despite having a relatively short career in Europe, was the first to substantially change how the art of illusion was performed. His legacy has been honoured among magicians, who consider him the "Father of Modern Magic", making him perhaps the more influential of the two.

Index

Glossary

choreography The art of arranging steps or movements in time to music

electromagnetism Study of the relationship between magnetic forces and electricity

escapology Methods and techniques of escaping from being confined or tied up

intellectual property The right to an original creative work, which can be protected by a patent

patent A legal document giving rights to the creator of an invention or other form of intellectual property

sleight of hand Skilful movements that make something happen without showing how it was done

therapeutic Something that helps to improve a person's physical or mental health

transposition When two or more things are made to change places